The Howling Dog

Tracey Campbell Pearson

Farrar Straus Giroux / New York

For Gregory
and for Mr. B.

It was nighttime.
The moon was up
and all was quiet in the town, until . . .

the Howling Dog began to bark.
She barked and she howled and she barked,
but no one came.

So, off she went
to visit the Weatherbees.

She woke up their dog, Wally,
and their cat, Winston.

She woke up the littlest Weatherbee, Sarah,

who woke up her big brother

and their mom and dad.
But still the Howling Dog barked.

She woke up the Burgs' chickens,
who woke up the Burgs.

She woke up Mrs. Gray's sheep,
who woke up Mr. Gray.

She woke up Farmer John's cows,
who woke up Farmer John
and his family.

Still the Howling Dog barked.

Soon the entire town was awake.

Then the Howling Dog was happy.
She was no longer lonely,

and she was quiet.

So Farmer John's cows went back to sleep,
and so did Farmer John
and his family.

Mrs. Gray's sheep went back to sleep,
and so did Mr. Gray.

The Burgs' chickens went back to sleep,

and so did the Burgs.

All the Weatherbees went back to sleep:
their dog, Wally,
their cat, Winston,
the littlest Weatherbee, Sarah,
Sarah's big brother,
and their mom and dad.

Finally, the entire town was sound asleep,

and this time,

so was the Howling Dog.